I0552091

Sweet Lifts

The Adventures of Miriam the Thief

Carolyn Ivy Stein

Published by Jeweled Sea Press, 2022.

This is a work of fiction. Similarities to real people, places, or events are entirely coincidental.

SWEET LIFTS

First edition. January 8, 2022.

ISBN: 978-1737018797

Written by Carolyn Ivy Stein.

Table of Contents

To Steve, the love of my life

Meet Miriam the Thief and Friends

I first met Miriam when she sauntered onto a frozen Memphis street with a hot dreidel burning a hole in her purse. By the time that first story ended (published in WMG's Holiday Spectacular 2021) I knew I wanted to spend more time in her world.

Miriam, a kind-hearted thief, who usually steals from the filthy rich to sell to the morally deficient rich, is always ready for a new adventure. This collection of short stories explores her relationships: with her team, with her family, and with strangers who appear needing her help.

I've written these five stories to explore Miriam and the most important relationships in her life. In these pages, you'll meet her family, her mentor, a few members of her team, and a fleeting encounter with a mysterious stranger who nevertheless knows Miriam's soul.

It all began when Kris Rusch suggested I turn in a holiday story for the Holiday Spectacular. It didn't seem possible. I don't even celebrate Christmas. Hanukkah isn't quite the same. I worried about the problem of Hanukkah until one day Miriam appeared with a hot dreidel in downtown Memphis, ready for adventure.

The story came out sweet and fast and left open the potential for more adventure and a sweet love affair. My biggest regret was that I'd left Miriam behind as I went on to write other stories. But now she's back for more fun and games.

I plan to write a novel or novella starring Miriam the Thief, which is part of why I wrote these stories, to meet the people around Miriam. Some of them will surely appear in Miriam's further adventures.

In this book you'll find five stories that explore Miriam's relationships.

Hour of the Puppy

When Miriam's father barricades himself in his house, Miriam heads to rural New Mexico for some breaking and entering in a good cause.

Letters of Love and Larceny

Crosby just wants to spend his off-hours forging famous love letters for his girlfriend. When his jerk of a boss orders him into the office in the wee hours of the morning, the day before he plans to propose, Crosby finds someone else is interested in pens, letters, and him: Miriam the Thief.

The Train Job

No way would Miriam turn down a free trip on the fabled *City of New Orleans* train, even if she has to plan a heist while riding it. The only other two passengers in her car have their own agendas. Miriam features in their plans despite her efforts to focus on the heist plan.

Five-Fingered Teamwork

Running the Albuquerque Bosque and timing her next theft, Miriam finds Jessie crumpled on the boardwalk, her face a mess of bruises. Sometimes all anyone needs is a little help.

Passing the Torch

A mysterious text message from a suspicious source sends Miriam racing back to Memphis to rescue her friend and mentor, whether he wants to be rescued or not.

I love Miriam. She's not only brave, competent, and daring, she's also a great friend. I hope you will enjoy meeting her as much as I have.

Carolyn Ivy Stein

Hour of the Puppy

Two am: the hour of the wolf, the art thief and of all predators prowling the night.

Normally, Miriam loved this time of night. The world was quiet, the air thick and warm, like a blanket enfolding Memphis. It was her time to sit with a mug of warm salty broth and make her plans while sipping the soothing broth. But tonight, Miriam felt she was hung together with bailing wire made of anxiety and fear.

She returned her attention to the large map of the Corvasce Museum in Cleveland spread out across her wooden dining room table. She tried to concentrate, to focus. Her agent had marked the security cameras and motion detectors he knew about with red dots. But he couldn't know everything, which was why Miriam was going to visit it herself. She could see he'd missed a few that had to be there. It was clear this museum was using the Stewart-Gardner method, which meant there had to be additional cameras over the doors pointing up. She marked them in purple ink. She took another sip of the broth, savoring the umami taste.

The phone rang and Miriam jumped. Two in the morning, Memphis time, meant that it was one in the morning in Albuquerque. Eva and Debs had not stopped calling, even though she'd agreed to fly out to check in on her father. She considered avoiding the phone call and pretending she asleep. But they would know it for the lie it was. Miriam had always been a night owl, which just went to show she was born to be a cat burglar.

The phone buzzed. Her watch vibrated against her wrist in time with the phone. Miriam sighed. There was no hope for it but to answer the call. She needed to reassure her sisters that she would be there tomorrow with a Shabbat dinner for their father and would convince him to let her in. But no matter what, she would not Zoom with them to strategize. Not after last time.

She checked the phone, wondering if it was Eva or Debs this time. Or perhaps they'd enlisted one of her nieces. But she didn't recognize the number. Chances were, no scam caller was calling at 2am, which meant it was probably an emergency of some sort. Of course, it was.

"Hello?"

"Miriam, I need help." It was Abby. Her voice sounded strange, and Miriam's skin tingled as adrenaline surged through her. Last she'd heard, Abby had gotten out of prison six months ago and seemed happy and excited to start on a new life. Abby told Marianne that she wouldn't ever go back to smuggling. No way was she going back to jail. A waste of talent in Miriam's opinion. A damned shame. Abby was one of the best in the business where when it came to moving merch. But everyone had to find their own place of peace and happiness. Until this moment, she'd figured that Abby found hers on the right side of the street.

"Abby, what's wrong?" she asked.

Abbey choked back a sob. "I need a place to stay. Just for a night or two. I can't—I can't talk about it right now."

"Are you being chased? If you are, I can find you a safe house. Otherwise, come to my place. I'm on a plane tomorrow morning. You can stay here while I'm gone."

"Miriam, you are the best, the absolute best friend anyone could ever have! Are you going on a job? I mean, do you need help?" Her voice lilted a bit as if hoping she could join Miriam on the museum job.

"No, unfortunately. Family business. No one knows where my father is, or rather, everyone knows where he is. But he won't leave the house. Or let anyone in. So, I am the one who has to get him out and find out what's wrong."

"What about your sisters?"

"He won't answer their calls or let anyone in."

"Oh, that sounds bad."

"If you want to hang out here, come right over. It will be good to have someone here, you know, in case of theft."

Abby laughed. No one had better security than Miriam. She could defeat most locks and security systems. She'd set up her own security with multiple levels. Defense in depth. Miriam thought of it as several perimeter walls around Fortress Miriam. But the greatest protection from both police and thieves was that she didn't keep anything valuable in her home.

Abby arrived, looking like she'd been crying all night. Her face was splotchy, and the whites of her eyes were strung with red. She had no makeup on and looked quite a bit worse for the wear. She even had a new scar running along the side of her cheek, something that she must've acquired in prison since Miriam didn't remember it.

Miriam set up tea. She moved the map aside to make room for her two best tea mugs, setting aside the one with the cat astronaut to cheer Abby and keeping her second favorite for herself. Hers had a group of puppies sitting in a basket with the words "Mornings are Ruff" across the top. She folded the tablecloth over the map to retain some security against casual eyes.

Abby arrived in a loud cacophony of knocking. Once in the kitchen she slumped into one of the hard wooden cafe chairs. She stared down at the dark liquid in her cup but barely touched the mug or sipped the strong tea.

Seeing her friend in this state brought a deep sense of foreboding. Before prison, Abby had been a happy-go-lucky soul. One of those blessed with the view that life is a party and she had to try everything. Prison hadn't beaten that out of her but whatever had happened lately seemed to have broken something in her friend. Miriam squeezed Abby's hand in a reassuring way and stared into her eyes in what she hoped was a reassuring manner. "Abby, tell me what's wrong."

"Pretty much everything." She stared at Miriam's hand over her own, barely seeming to register it before meeting Miriam's eyes. "I got out of prison about six months ago. I've been living with my sister and her husband ever since. Can't seem to get a job. Can't do anything. And now my brother-in-law tossed me out. Says I'm not trying. But I am."

A trickle of tears began. Miriam grabbed a box of tissues from a nearby table and waited.

"I don't know what to do. Can I stay here, just for a night or two?"

"What sort of work do you want to do?" Miriam asked, thinking rapidly over the jobs she had and whether she could use a someone to move the merch.

"I don't know, Miriam. I still want to go straight. But no one seems to want to make that easy on me. Or even possible. I just need a place to crash for the night and sleep on it."

"Didn't they train you in something in prison?"

"Not much. We spent some time training animals. But I'll tell you, the guards thought the real animals were us. It was so hard. I never want to return. Can I just stay?" Her lip trembled.

Miriam patted Abby's hand. "My house is your house. At least for a few days. I'm heading to Albuquerque tomorrow. Stay here. Rest. Think. When I get back, we'll talk more."

THE DRY AIR SUCKED the moisture from Miriam's skin and the altitude, so much higher in Albuquerque than Memphis, made each step feel a bit heavier. She was glad she didn't live here full time. She'd have to bathe in moisturizer.

When she'd arrived in Albuquerque, Miriam found a relatively new Ford Taurus Eva had arranged for her. She had told her sister not to bother getting her a rental car, intending to pick up a car on her own and getting some necessary practice with wiring an engine. She didn't do enough to keep in practice with car theft. But Eva had said that it was the least she could do.

It was a comfy car and Miriam especially appreciated the large hatchback which was filled right now with food she'd picked up at Whole Foods for Shabbat. Plus, she'd brought a challah from Ricki's Cookies in Memphis, the best challah in the world. Upon hearing that Miriam would see her father again, Rikki had bundled a dozen of her famous chocolate chip cookies in with the challah and told her to send her best wishes to her family.

Miriam hoped the roasted chicken, the miso soup, and that packet of sides she'd found in the deli case at Whole Foods would be enough of a temptation that her father would not mind when she let herself into his house. And if he did, the cookies would be the perfect peace offering. The roasted chicken alone might be enough. It smelled fantastic.

The plan was for Miriam to drive up to the front of her father's house, get him to let her in, and then contact her sisters so that they could stage an intervention.

Eva had said, "Daddy always lets you in. You're his favorite."

He had little a choice. Miriam thought. She actually let herself in. No lock could keep her out.

But with everything that Eva and Debs had said, she was worried.

It wasn't like dad to shut everyone out.

Their mother had left the United States a year ago. Even though her parents were divorced, they had a good relationship and saw each other weekly. But her mother had left for an expedition to Prague, and no one had heard much from her that couldn't fit on a postcard. Her father seemed to be OK with it, but at a loss.

Deb's theory was that her father had taken up with some floozy, and that's what was going on in the house. In her more imaginative moments, she suggested he was conducting nonstop orgies.

Miriam discounted this. She couldn't imagine her meek sweet father opening his home to orgies or even be attracted to a floozy. Now her mother, that was a different question.

If Debs had suggested that her mother was having orgies or hosting orgies or going to orgies, that would have been right in line with her character.

Eva was not taken with the floozy theory. She thought their father was depressed. She'd said he needed his daughters, all of them, to come and reassure him that he was loved, and they need him in their lives. So, Eva came up with the idea of the intervention. Debs had gone along saying that she had always wanted to interrupt their parents in an orgy and if it was only Dad, well, that would be fun too.

Dad's house was down a dry gravel road just north and east of Placitas. The dust swirled in eddies around her car as she drove up Jackalope Road, laughing to herself at the name. Thankfully, her GPS had been updated in this car because otherwise she didn't know how she would ever have found it.

The house was in a new subdivision, with large lots of land big enough for horses or hiking or whatever one did in the wilderness.

The house itself looked like any other suburban home in Albuquerque, albeit a lot larger. It was made of pinkish stucco with a stone and stucco wall around it. As she brought the car to a halt, what sounded like a hundred dogs barked at her. She checked the front door, giving the handle a little jiggle, but it was locked. On the door in her father's handwriting a sign read, "Shhh! Babies are sleeping. Go away! Leave packages here."

Hmmm. Babies are sleeping. What babies? Had her father started a daycare center? If so, those dogs were going to wake the babies more than a quiet thief knocking or ringing the doorbell.

No one came to the door, and the dogs settled down after a bit. It was probably easier for everyone if she just picked the lock.

She made quick work of the locks, which were nothing special, just a brass door lock and a Patriot deadbolt. They practically purred as she worked her picks on them and let herself in.

A wave of odors reached her nose as she did, wet dog, dirty diapers, and something she couldn't identify but made her nose wrinkle up in distaste. The entryway had a playpen filled with a pile of fuzzy black and white puppies and what looked like the weary mother, a brown and tan dog with a long, elegant nose softly resting on one of the fat puppies.

As she walked across the reddish Saltillo tile, her feet moved silently in what Josh, her mentor, called her assassin slippers. She found more and more enclosures with litters of puppies. The entire house was filled with dogs.

She checked the kitchen and bathrooms until she finally came upon her father wearing a blue bathrobe and holding two fuzzy brown puppies, one cupped in each massive hand. He held them close to his face.

"First, you," he said, looking the fatter puppy in the eyes and shaking him lightly. "Stop biting your brother. You have to learn to be nice to each other."

He let the puppy down near his feet and the mewling things crawled on top of his shoes and peed. He held the other puppy up to his face. "You need to learn to defend yourself. He is just going to keep at it if you don't." He set the other puppy on the ground near his brother, whose tail he promptly bit, starting a race across the kitchen floor.

Her father turned and, as he did, he saw Miriam. His eyes widened. "What are you doing here?"

"Apparently interrupting your bonding moments. Dad, what's going on? What's with all the puppies?"

His head lifted in a challenging way. "Do you have a problem with puppies?"

"Does anyone? I mean the portion of the internet that isn't cat pictures is puppy pictures."

"The world is cruel. We rescued all of these sweethearts from terrible people who were hurting them or abandoning them." He brushed away something that looked suspiciously like a tear. "So..." He motioned the house generally. "Here we are."

"Daddy, you can't just take in strays. What are you going to do once you run out of space?

"I have a plan for that. I'm building a structure out back. I think I can fit another 5 to 10 litters of puppies depending on how big the litters are and how big the puppies are..." His voice trailed off, but Miriam could see he had the same look he always did when he was doing mental math. "And then if we can get the others adopted will have plenty of room again."

Miriam looked around the house and realized there was no way she could bring Eva in here for an intervention. Her neat sister would freak out at the idea of her father living in a mess of peeing and pooping puppies. So instead, she said to her father "I brought Shabbat dinner. "Eva and Debs want to eat with you too, but let's just make this the two of us.

Her father laughed. "Maybe the 40 of us."

"Are there 40 dogs? How are you affording dog food?"

Her father looked down at his shoes. She took in his slender frame, more emaciated than usual and she knew the answer. "You're not eating. You can't give all your food to the puppies."

"I'm eating," he said defensively. "I have a good meal every day. I don't need charity and I don't need more food than that."

Miriam could see that she was not going to win this argument. Her personal belief was that there is no point in fighting if unless you could win, but she couldn't bring her sisters into the house.

"Daddy I brought Shabbat dinner and enough for the two of us and enough for leftovers. Perfect challah from Ricki's Cookies and some cookies she threw in for free. She misses you. You should phone her. Shall we eat?"

It looked like she was about to win over her father when suddenly the door opened. Debs entered, her hair perfectly coiffed and wearing a mustard yellow designer suit. she stumbled into the kitchen dropping a book with the title, *Grieving and the Newly Single Man*. She knelt to retrieve it "Good God Daddy! Dogs? You've gone to the dogs? Literally? How does anyone explain this? What will people say? If anyone finds out that my father is a cat lady, er, dog man..." She threw up her hands dramatically to emphasize the impossibility of being known as the dog man's daughter. "Daddy, I just got a position on the board. Don't embarrass me."

"Out! Out! Both of you. I will not be spoken to in that way. I am still your father."

One of the puppies ran over to Debs. She squeaked, tried to dodge it, succeeding only in stepping on a paw.

The puppy gazed up at her in confusion as it piddled on the floor next to her feet.

Debs "This is impossible! Impossible!"

"Hush Debs. This was your idea. Remember? You wanted to see what was going on."

"I thought it was orgies, not puppies!"

Her father picked up the cowering puppy, cooing gently at it until it looked a bit less fraught. He motioned to a mop and bucket of water in the corner. "Miriam. Clean the floor next to your sister. Debs, you are scaring the puppies. Stop yelling."

For a moment the only noise came from the puppies.

"Orgies? What has your mother been saying about me? There was only one. And it wasn't my idea."

"Daddy, I've flown all the way from Memphis to bring you Shabbat. Surely you can let me serve it tonight."

Over dinner, she got the entire story out of her father. He found the first set of puppies under a porch: two already dead, three in mortal peril from disease, and two who were the only true survivors of that litter. He took them home, warmed them, tried to help. But he was at a loss, so he called a dog rescue service he found on the Internet, and they agreed to help him. But he learned this was just the barest drop in the ocean. There were so many more puppies abandoned, harmed, and maltreated.

"I couldn't do nothing," he said. "Right?"

Mariam thought for a moment and then shook her head. "Yes, you're right. But you can't take in all the litters in the world, Daddy. You can't even handle these. They are running you ragged."

"And they're peeing everywhere," Debs added.

Eva nodded in agreement. "It's unsanitary."

"I know that, but as long as I have room to take in more, I have to. I just don't know what to do with them as they get older."

"That's a good question." And then she had an idea. She dialed Abby. "Hey Abby, how are you doing? I have a question for you. Maybe an opportunity."

Abby's voice was apologetic. "About that, Miriam," she said. "I know I said that I would really appreciate a job with you. But I've reconsidered. I just can't. I need to stay clean. I can't go back to jail. I just can't."

"Don't worry, you're not going to go to jail."

"You won't go to jail because you're good, but I'm not good enough," she said. "I've proven that already. I'm really bad at this."

"No, no," Miriam said. "You're misunderstanding. I have a question for you. What is it that you were trained for in the prison?"

"Training service dogs," she said. "But it's of no use. No one will hire me. The state won't even give me a license to open my own place because I'm an ex-con. It seems as if they just want me to die or to never be able to work."

"Are you be willing to relocate for a job?

"Relocate?"

"Relocate?" Her father echoed.

"You have a problem," she said, pointing to her father. "You have too many dogs. Then she turned to the phone. "And you, Abby, have a problem. You can't find dogs to train. But here we are. I have dogs that need training."

"It's not that easy, Miriam." Abby protested. "You have to start them young like when they're puppies."

"I have 40 puppies and a man who can get a license and hire you. He's offering room and board, plus a small stipend once Debs convinces her foundation to support the operation. Right?"

Debs shrugged uncertainly.

"Who is that?" Her father asked pointing at the phone.

"The person who is going to save your dogs and your daughters' sanity," she said. She handed the phone over to her father, saying to Abby, "Abby, this is my father. He is adopting puppies—"

"Fostering puppies," her father corrected.

Miriam nodded and started again. "Abby, this is my father. He is fostering puppies who have no future without you. And I think your future will be brighter as well. Surely the two of you can come to some accommodation." She explained the situation to Abby and handed the phone to her father.

HER FATHER'S NEW DINING room, cleared of puppies, turned out to be quite beautiful with long picture windows displaying the New Mexico terrain with scrubby trees and yellow grass. It was like a living Georgia O'Keefe painting. Eva's two children and Glynnis, Debs' sober eleven-year-old, were playing with the puppies in the living room but when Debs called to them, they all filed in and took their places.

Abby had inserted extra leaves into the large wooden table and helped set the table with plates for twelve. The last six weeks had transformed her. Her cheeks glowed, and she seemed to always be smiling. Perhaps the prison knew what it had been about training her to train dogs. She was a natural with them.

Across the walls were pictures of the dogs drawn by children from Glynnis' classroom who came to visit the puppies once a week to help with their care.

Abby couldn't do it all, nor could Miriam's father, as they both pointed out. But a class of children who were excited to help with the puppies, Abby's expertise, Deb's foundation, and her father's enormous heart were enough. At least for now.

Debs said she couldn't bear to enter the house if it smelled like a dog shelter, so Debs and Eva paid a house cleaner to come weekly to keep the place up. Every Friday afternoon, before the sun set, a cleaner came.

The sisters shared Shabbat duty, each bringing food each week, leaving their father no excuse to pour all his grocery money into puppy chow. For a while, there were no worries about puppy food since Abby found several bags of dog food that had "fallen off a truck" and were being unloaded at a great price. She was still the best at moving merch, even when the merch was legal (mostly).

As to Miriam, she moved to Albuquerque. After all, she could plan her jobs on any old table. But she couldn't keep an eye on her family from so far away.

As the sun set over the horizon, changing the color of the sky from brilliant blue to shades of pink, red, and dark blue, Eva, Debs, and Miriam stood up and moved to the head of the table where a pair of brass candlesticks with white candles were waiting. The challah, from Whole Foods this time, was covered with a cross-stitched cover showing two dogs with their paws over their eyes saying the blessings over the bread. Deb's husband, Lev, brought a couple of bottles of wine, which he poured for everyone.

Eva struck a match. As she lit the Shabbat candles, they began the ancient prayer. The smell of sulfur and melted paraffin scented the air, mingling with the savory smells of soup, chicken, and an oat and bean loaf for the vegans. A howl went up outside. Miriam liked to think that the dogs also welcomed the Sabbath Queen in their own way.

"Shabbat Shalom. May peace fill every heart, whether that heart be human or canine," she said.

"Amen," responded everyone around the table.

The Train Job

The train bumped, rattled, and swayed pleasantly along as Miriam snuggled into the large, padded seat reading through the file on her lap and sipping from the aromatic chicory coffee she brought with her.

There was no one else in her car except a man two seats behind her wearing, of all things, a grayish red ski hat with a grubby hand-knitted scarf in the middle of summer and an old woman in a crisp, white Mennonite cap with a long dark blue dress seated ahead of her near the exit. The elder moved her crochet hook so fast through the pile of yarn on her lap, that it seemed as if she were moving at the speed of the train. Miriam guessed some lucky baby would have a warm wrapper before the train stopped in Memphis.

The scenery slipped by, a green plain filled with cotton fields and rice paddies on her side and a dense forest of trees hung with kudzu vines on the other, as the train moved through Louisiana on the way to Memphis. Miriam couldn't help but hum Arlo Guthrie's song that immortalized the *City of New Orleans* in her head. But she wasn't there as tourist. She was there because Josh had said it was time for a train job.

She'd laughed when he said that. It wasn't the Wild West anymore and her skills definitely didn't include climbing on the roof of a train while fighting the bad guy of the week. Fanciful, is what it was. She'd told him so. But she wasn't likely to turn down a free trip on the fabled *City of New Orleans* train.

In some ways it had disappointed. She'd pictured something ornately beautiful, like the pictures of the Orient Express, but this was a rather ordinary train with a flat blue and gray carpeting shot through with lines of white. Gray and steel Formica tables in the club car provided a working and eating area. She'd just come from there. She'd spent her time eating an uninspired breakfast of oatmeal and coffee while filling in the details on her map of the club car.

Miriam's job was to case the place. In about a month the Spanish Museum of the Working Souls would send a shipment of art, books, and one small sacred pin in a box of miscellany. Miriam was here for the sacred pin. Or at least she would be in in a month when it came time to take it. Today she was simply learning the train and enjoying the special perks of being a thief for hire.

The man in the ski cap swayed up the aisle. A bulge in his pocket betrayed the gun there. She cast her eyes down, as if she were studying something incredibly interesting, but it didn't work. The man swung into the seat next to her, pulled the folder from her hands, and shuffled through the annotated train car diagrams. "You one of them train enthusiasts?"

Miriam took him in. He dressed like a bum, but he smelled good with some expensive cologne. Too good. So not an undercover cop who would know better. Some other cop? Or just a jerk. She said coolly, "Maybe. Are you?"

"Nah, I'm a cop," he said. His teeth were clean white and perfect in his mouth, like a toothpaste model. But his cold eyes seemed to hunger, with an indecent eagerness. Some cruelty there, she thought. He pulled out a badge in a small leather case and flashed it at her, but too fast for her to be sure. Which could mean that it wasn't true, of course. Or that he just enjoyed playing with his prey before he ate it.

Her skin grew cold, and her heart stepped up its beat. But she didn't let it show. He was one of those guys who clearly enjoyed being a predator. If he hadn't become a cop, he would have been one of the bad dudes working the streets.

She forced herself to relax into the seat. "Is that so? Are you one of those railroad cops I've heard about? One of those guys looking for people riding without tickets?"

"I'm looking for you, Miriam Delacruz."

"That's not my name."

"Maybe not, but it was. Don't blame you for changing it. Don't blame you a bit. Had it been me who destroyed that man, I think I would have done the same. You take care of yourself like a sane girl and I don't see no reason to let anyone know you were here. You get me?" He fanned himself with the folder as if daring her to take it back.

She crossed her arms and glared at him. "I am working. Please return to your own seat and put down my property. My past is none of your business."

He smirked at her. "I think, Miriam, that it's time for you to stop working. Take a bit of me time. Avoid the cascade of trouble coming your way. Take my advice. As a friend."

He placed the folder down, laying his meaty hand on top of it, and brought his face close enough to hers that she could smell the cherry candy he'd been sucking. Too close for comfort, but she didn't flinch. He was trying to intimidate her and she'd be damned if that was going to happen. Better men than he had tried and failed. He lowered his voice adding a hiss of menace. "Get off this train."

She gave him her pious synagogue smile. "Thank you, sir. I believe I will do just that. Mr....?" She let her voice trail off uncertainly.

The man nodded. "You can call me Blakesworth. Glad you're being reasonable. He leaned back in the seat, removed his hand from the folder, dug around in his jacket pocket, and offered her a "snack-sized" package of gummy bears that looked like it had been in his pocket since last Halloween. "No hard feelings?"

"Indeed not," she said, ignoring the gummy bears and snatched the file folder. He sighed as she stowed it in her tote. She made a show of turning away from him, then wiggled her fingers at him and slid them into his pocket coming out with the gummy bears, which she waved at him, playfully slapping his face while pulling out his police badge with her other hand and pocketing it in a quick pickpocket slip and slide maneuver. Served the jerk right if he lost it. "I'll get off at my stop and not a moment sooner. Now if you would please leave me be. I have work to do."

The man growled deep in his throat, but he moved away, though not without a quick pat at the gun bulge in his pants. "You consider what I said. Safer for you. Safer for everyone." With that he swayed back to his seat

The man made her nervous. One thing she knew for sure, though. He wasn't a cop. Former cop, maybe. Someone working his own string, probably. Dangerous? Certainly. She would check his 'badge' later.

Moments like this Miriam wished she packed a gun. She didn't and not just because being caught as a burglar while packing a gun meant an automatic extension of jail time. It was mostly because she had no intention of killing anyone. Her father once told her that the only reason to draw a gun was to kill someone or some other creature. And each time you did it, you lost a piece of your soul. Miriam figured she needed all of her soul she had left.

She buried her nose in her cup, taking a few calming breaths. Her coffee had cooled but she still enjoyed the cedar scent of the chicory and the bitter chocolate aroma of the coffee. No one did coffee better than New Orleans. Then she pulled the folder from her bag. Just six hours left on the train and in that time she needed to figure out where the art would be stored, how best to liberate the sacred pin, where to hide it, and potential escape routes.

What she really needed was an expert in trains. But they weren't exactly falling off the trees into her lap. She focused on the map of the club car. It was unwise to conduct a theft in front of a room filled with people, which made it unexpected. She considered the placement of the seats. Could she install a keeper box below one of them? Perhaps when she made the trip back to New Orleans in a week?

But she couldn't know whether the train would be the same one. Still, as a potential back up plan, that had possibilities. She made a note.

A rustling near her pulled her out of her reverie. The Mennonite lady was standing next to her holding her bag of yarn. "Excuse me, so sorry to interrupt you."

Who knew trains were such social places? Miriam repressed a sigh. She smiled up at the woman, who probably just needed some company. "No problem. What can I do for you?"

The woman pointed a wrinkled, freckled hand at the seat recently vacated by the jerk. "Mind if I sit with you? Two women alone, well, if we sat together we wouldn't be alone." She smiled and it lit her eyes like tiny candles of warmth and happiness.

"Sure. Have a seat." Miriam braced herself for the conversation that would inevitably follow. Six hours left to learn everything about this train. But the woman was clearly alone and elderly. Miriam could afford an hour to chat.

The woman sat down lightly, with more physical grace than Miriam expected. She must exercise. Or do Mennonite women do farm work? Or was that just the Amish women? Miriam didn't know.

The woman picked up her crochet hook and a soft pastel blue yarn and started looping it over the hook. "Thank you, kindly. I'm Helena. I believe I heard your name is Miriam? Is that right?"

"Yes. It's good to meet you Helena."

"Yours is a lovely name. So biblical. But look at me babbling on. Don't worry. I won't interrupt your work. I can see that you have serious concerns ahead." She bent her head to her work, which was not at all what Miriam had expected.

"Are you making a baby blanket for a new grandson?" Miriam asked. "It's beautiful."

"This? Thank you. The premature infant floor of our local hospital needs blankets. Poor sweet things, so young and vulnerable. We've adopted the floor. Each of us is putting together a kit for a child. We all offer what we can. Just as you do."

Miriam nodded.

"I am your contact, you know," the woman said in a low conspiratorial voice, her head angled down as if she could quiet the words by speaking them into her yarn. "If you need anything in furtherance of your mission, I'm here for you. I know this train better than anyone, even better than the conductor, I think. Though he's a good boy."

"You're here for me?"

The woman nodded firmly. "I cannot bear to think what will happen to that precious, precious life if we cannot rescue her before the train arrives in Jackson."

"I think you've mistaken me for someone else." Miriam said. But her mind swirled with the implications. That's what Blakesworth must have meant. Years ago on a job to steal a small statuette, she'd removed a child from a terrible situation. Then she'd made her own situation worse by testifying about what she saw so that the child wasn't returned to those monsters. Who turned out to be mobbed up. She'd washed her identity as best she could afterward. Apparently not good enough. Damn!

"Nonsense. I saw your floor plans. You are planning a heist. What else is of greater value on this train than a woman's life? I reported the situation to our mutual friends and here you are." The woman patted her hand and spoke soothingly. "I know I am not quite what you expected. God places us where we can do the most good, no matter our age. So it is in this case."

God Almighty! She'd wished for a train specialist to fall into her lap, and here one was. But with her own extra mission. "Helena, I was, er, not fully briefed by our mutual friend. Can you fill me in?"

Helena smiled warmly and explained the situation in terse, quick sentences. Reading between the lines, Miriam figured out that, "our mutual friend" was an organization that rescued missing people given up on by the conventional authorities, though she wasn't sure what Helena did for them. Nor could she figure out whether it was a private group, a religious group, or a governmental agency. What Helena was most keen to get across was that the woman had been lost after the group rescued her once before. She was somewhere on the train and Helena thought she could find her but not extract her.

"We just need to get the poor lady to our agents in Jackson, Mississippi. They'll get her back to her people from there." Helena picked up speed with her crochet hook. The silvery blue of the hook and the soft blue of the mounting length of the blanket was hypnotic.

And who are her people? Does she even want to go back to them? But Miriam didn't voice those questions. She would ask the woman herself. After all, the woman can't want to be transferred around like a piece of luggage on the train. She should have a choice in what happened to her.

They'd just passed Hammond, LA. How much time did that give them? Miriam tried to figure it out in her head before realizing that the whole point of having a train expert was to get answers like that. She tapped Helena on the shoulder. "How much time does that give us?"

"Mmmm." Helena looked up and to the left before returning to Miriam's face. "About two hours, maybe another half hour. Depends. Train isn't always reliable."

Miriam opened the pack of gummy bears and offered Helena one of them. They were good, fruity and chewy for all that the bag seemed old. "OK, if I'm understanding this, we have to find a woman who may or may not be willing to come with us, pull her out of a situation she can't get out of, and then hide her long enough to get her to Jackson, Mississippi? Is that about the size of it?"

Helena's eyes glowed with satisfaction. "Exactly! So what is our plan?"

"I'm the one with the plan?"

"They always send an experienced agent for me to work with."

Miriam cleared her throat. Right. Well, it can't be that different to free a woman than it is to free a piece of art, right? Same process, though perhaps more brownie points with the Almighty.

Miriam opened her folder and pulled out her sketches and plans of the train. "Show me where you think she is." She handed a pen to Helena who began drawing on the pages and explaining the various potential hiding spots.

"This one," She pointed to a place on the map that had nothing particularly interesting. "This is a little closet under the stairs. It's hard to get to, especially for adults. If the woman is small enough, they could have her here. It's close enough to the tracks that we wouldn't be able to hear her even if she screamed."

"You think that they'd put her in there without a guard of some sort? It looks like it would be too small for even a very small woman and a big burly guard." She chewed another gummy bear letting the sweetness fill her mouth.

Helena puckered her lips. "If it was an equally small woman guard, they could fit. My sisters and I used to hide in one just like it. No one ever found us." She tilted her head sideways and laughed. "Though to tell you the truth, I'm not sure my parents looked all that hard. We were a noisy bunch."

Miriam looked at the map again, memorized the location, and stood up. She said loudly to Helena, "You are just a delight, but I need the restroom. Be right back."

"Take these," Helena said, "pressing a wooden set of knitting needles in her palm. You never know when crafts will come in handy."

Miriam paced briskly down the corridor, swaying with the train. Looking back she saw Blakesworth start to follow her, his hand on the bulge in his pants. Damn!

She could go down to the restroom, but she had a feeling he would wait outside it, or worse, come in. She didn't want to be alone with him. Proceed to the club car? He would chase her all over the train.

She heard a loud crash behind her. Blakesworth had fallen near Helena who was saying, "Oh dear! Oh dear! I'm so sorry. I'm so clumsy with my yarn. Oh whoops!"

Miriam suppressed a laugh as she ran down the stairway, down the lower hall and then searched for the secret door.

It was where Helena had said it would be.

No problem, then. This would be easy. She just needed to watch for guards, help the woman out of the steel-encased closet, and find a place to hide her until Jackson, Mississippi.

Miriam crouched down, hiding in the shadowed hallway, curling herself into the smallest possible shape. And waited.

No one came, either from the little door or from the stairs.

She pressed herself against the steel door, listening as best she could for sounds of conversation or calls for help.

Nothing. Just the smell of iron and dust, the roar of the wheels against the tracks, and the great rumbling vibration this close to the bottom of the train.

Well she couldn't wait forever. And Helena swore that there wasn't another opening to this closet. Though how long ago Helena had been a child hiding, she couldn't guess.

She knocked on the door.

Hearing nothing, she wiggled the knob, but it was locked.

She knelt down, pulled out the multi-lockpick jackknife she kept discreetly tucked in her bra near the underwire where it wouldn't attract the attention of metal detectors. The lock yielded grumpily to her ministrations. In that moment she knew that no one was inside. The lock clearly hadn't been opened in years.

Sure enough, the small compartment had a set of boxes, which Miriam moved aside just in case someone had been hidden behind them. But no one had. And as far as Miriam could determine the boxes were filled with forgotten supplies from the late 1980s. At another time, it would have been fascinating to go through this spot. She made a note to do just that when she stowed the sacred pin here next month.

Miriam smiled. God sent her the perfect train expert. Now Miriam just needed to do her part and rescue the abducted woman. The scales had to balance.

Miriam closed the door and relocked it. She'd return at her leisure and prepare the spot for the heist. But now to find the woman.

She struggled to remember the other places Helena marked on the map as possibilities. She could return to Helena, but she was free of Blakesworth now and she wanted it to remain that way. A systematic search of the potential spots had the advantage of being thorough. And the disadvantage of perhaps taking too long or alerting the wrong people that she was on the hunt.

She briefly considered how much easier it would be if she were an old west super thief who could run along the top of a moving train. Good sense prevailed, though. She decided to start with the most unlikely spot next, the galley pantry closet. It would mean that the abductors were using an inside man. It was so audacious that it was the one place no one would consider. It was possible that there was more than one insider as part of the kidnappers.

The place was busiest at dinner, which would be Miriam's preferred time since so many people provided natural distractions. But they were likely to arrive in Jackson right in the middle of the dinner rush. The woman had to be rescued before that.

She would just have to improvise. Afterall, sometimes you can do impossible things through great daring, moving too fast for fate to catch. Too much caution gave the enemy the first move.

When Miriam arrived at the dining car, it was almost empty. One of the stewards was wiping down a table with a strong-smelling ammonia solution before covering it with a white tablecloth. A man sat at a nearby table with a half-eaten bacon and cheese sandwich and a glass of iced tea. She didn't see anyone else. The smell of garlic roasted chicken emanated from the kitchen.

She took the table nearest the kitchen and pretended to study the menu while taking in the situation.

Normally, there were two servers and an unknown number of people in the kitchen hidden away. Today there was just the one server, an older woman with a comfortable layer of fat and her black and gray hair up in a bun. She was humming to herself.

Miriam couldn't tell if there were more people in the kitchen, but no upside to hesitation now.

As the server passed her table, Miriam slid as gracefully as she could on a train that was taking turns and swaying. Her stomach flipped over when the train jerked as she grabbed the server from behind, pressed the business end of the knitting needles into her back and whispered, "Don't make me hurt you. Keep quiet and do what I tell you to do." She pressed the needles a bit harder into the woman's back, hoping it felt like a knife.

The woman froze. "I did everything you told me. Please don't hurt me. Please."

Now that was interesting. The server was involved, clearly. But an unwilling participant perhaps? What had she been made to do? Miriam didn't have time to ask. Every minute meant more danger. If she were to outrun fate, she needed to be quick. "Open the pantry."

"It's locked."

"Then unlock it," Miriam hissed, her frustration leaking out.

"I don't have a key."

Miriam sighed and turned the woman around, glancing quickly at the man reading the book. He hadn't noticed them. She brought her lips close to the woman's ear again and spoke in her most menacing tone. "OK, here is what you are going to do. You are going to turn around, leave this car and go to the bathroom. Wait there."

"But I'm on duty."

Miriam dug the knitting needles in harder, her real frustration pushing her further than she intended this time.

The woman whimpered.

"Sorry," Miriam said pulling back a bit. "I'm giving you a break. Take it."

"Sure. Sure. I'm going. But what if someone steals the chocolate bars again?"

Miriam laughed. "They won't. Go. Now."

The woman moved as fast as Miriam had ever seen anyone move. Her balance on the careening car was amazing, especially for a woman of her age.

Miriam let herself into the servers' area and studied the pantry door. It was secured with a simple door lock meant to keep children out of the candy and not much more. Miriam jiggled her lock picks and the door opened with a squeak. It was almost a disappointment how easy it was.

She looked around to see if anyone had noticed her. The man at the table was yawning. In another moment, he might look up and see her. A stack of clean aprons sat the side. She pulled a bib apron over her head, tied the ribbons, and piled her hair into a hat.

The man looked up from his book.

Miriam waved to him with a friendly grin.

He nodded gravely, then resumed reading his book, which was one of the latest thrillers where a civilian gets caught up in a plot to thwart terrorists. Miriam had read it a month ago. She'd thought it unrealistic, especially the section where he'd learned safe cracking in an afternoon, but it was an enthralling read and that's all a thriller needed to be.

She slipped into the pantry where she found a woman curled in the darkest corner of the pantry, near a pile of giant cans of nacho cheese. Miriam palpated the woman's wrists and listened for her heart and breath. She wasn't conscious, but her heart still beat and her breathing was normal. Miriam used her phone's flashlight function to see what was going on. She'd been tied up, gagged, and in the dim light it looked like she was covered in dried blood. So not a willing traveler then.

Not a lot of time either.

Miriam dodged back to the service station, grabbed a steak knife and went back into the pantry to cut the ropes. It took longer than she thought it would.

As she worked, she spoke to the woman, urging her to wake up. But it didn't happen. Miriam was strong but carrying this woman across several train cars just wasn't in the cards. And Helena wouldn't be of much help.

She walked purposefully over to the man at the table, dug into her pocket for Blakeworth's badge and flashed it at him, hoping the badge was real enough since she hadn't had time to check it. "Special Agent Kate Wilhelm," she said in her most no-nonsense voice. "I'm requesting all due help from you right now. We have an emergency."

The man straightened up, his full attention on her. "What can I do, Officer?"

Channeling the FBI agents she'd seen on TV, Miriam gave the man a tight, professional look. "We have a kidnap victim. I'll need your help carrying her to safety. There may be some danger, but I believe we can handle it. We've had our eyes on you and I don't mind telling you, we are impressed."

"You have? You are?" It came out in a squeak. "I mean, I'm always willing to serve my country."

Between the two of them, they got the woman vertical and splashed cold water on her cheeks, cleaning off the blood. They carried her out of the dining car to the lower level bathroom.

"Thank you. write down your name for me and I'll put you in for a special civilian commendation."

Once the man left, Miriam secreted the woman in the ladies washroom and stayed with her until she was conscious and could assert that she wanted the rescue Helena was offering.

Almost a month later, when Miriam took the train from Memphis to New Orleans to prepare it for the heist, she found Helena in the same car, curled into the overstuffed gray vinyl chair knitting a new little blanket. This one in pink. She looked tired and much older than she had a month ago.

Miriam stopped near her and said, "Excuse me, may I sit next to you?"

Helena's smile transformed her face. "Miriam! Of course. Please do sit."

"Were our mutual friends able to help get the woman where she wanted to go?"

Helena nodded. "God provides. She is back with her husband and children with only a small nightmare in what we hope will be a long, happy life."

"Good!" Miriam said. She offered Helena a breath mint and popped one in her mouth as well, enjoying the cold sensation on her tongue.

Helena's crochet hook slowed a bit as she studied Miriam's face. "You did well for someone caught by surprise."

"You knew I hadn't been sent by our mutual friends?"

"On the contrary. You were sent by God as the answer to our prayers. I just knew this was your first mission. You are filled with grace, Miriam. Never forget that we are the Lord's hands in the world. He depends on our ingenuity and kindness. I hope you also received what you needed from me and from him."

Miriam thought of the hidden closet prepared for her first "train job" and nodded. "I did."

"You can join our society in truth if you want. Serve the greater good as an employee and not just as a freelancer."

"I'm more of an independent contractor, I think. But if you need my help, you can call my agent." She wrote down Josh's contact information then impulsively kissed the woman on the cheek, feeling in her velvety skin a good life, lived long and filled with grace.

Passing the Torch

The early November air was cold, almost biting, despite the blue sky that was a feature of living in Albuquerque. Shivering, Miriam zipped up the running jacket made of fabric that felt as if it were barely there. It lapped over her shorts giving her the slightest bit of protection from the cold air. Within an hour the sun would burn off the morning chill and she knew she'd be grateful she hadn't overdressed. The gold and red leaves of the cottonwood trees blazed against the cloudless blue sky as Miriam padded down the dirt path carved between the trees along the Rio Grande enjoying the mineral and milkweed scent and the soft wetness the Rio Grande imparted to the air that moisturized her mouth and nose.

The temperature changed dramatically as she moved from cool shade to warm sun and back again. Her phone buzzed in her pocket as her watch buzzed against her wrist. She glanced down at it. Probably just another come-on from the furniture store. The advantage of stealing furniture over buying it was that no one texted with superfluous sales. Downside: she couldn't secrete a piece of furniture in her pocket.

When she saw the text she stopped, walked into the woods growing thickest near the river and pulled out her phone, her heart beating in her chest. It was a text from Josh's phone, her agent. He never contacted her this way. Never. Said it was too dangerous. So either someone else texted her from his phone or some cop was using it to flush out the thieves. Either way, not good.

—Sending a friend to your place. Danny could use a good man and a good meal. Let me know when you get this message.

It was in the code they'd worked out, which was something of a relief. Not a cop, then. But he was in trouble, couldn't talk about it, couldn't reach the computer he used to connect to the dark web, and didn't want her to respond. And he wanted her to stay away.

Her heart prickled her. Josh was more than an agent. He was her friend and mentor. If he needed her, she should be there.

On the other hand, if he thought it too dangerous, she had to respect that as well. She reread the brief message. Nowhere did he use their code word for cops or the phrase that would tell her to get out of town. So, something was wrong for him personally.

He just expected her to sit on her tush and not do anything. Damn him. She wasn't a kid anymore. She didn't need to be protected from life.

She sat down on a log and pulled up a schedule for the flights between Albuquerque and Memphis, booked one for the late afternoon, and within a few hours was on the flight with her go bag with everything she needed for a fast escape under the seat.

Miriam arrived at the Memphis airport in a flurry of crowds. The week before Thanksgiving travel was crazy. She'd barely been able to get a ticket. Now she dutifully stood in line waiting with everyone else. At least she didn't have the excessive luggage most others seemed to be burdened with.

A sense of foreboding shivered inside her. What would Josh say? What if he couldn't say anything at all? He wasn't going to like her disobeying him.

Damn it, someone needed to take care of him. He had, as far as she knew, no close family. Which wasn't to say that he didn't have any family. He had an ex-wife and parents who stopped speaking to him the day they learned he was trans.

Josh had made his own family. Bringing people together, giving of himself, forming community were all things he excelled at. Back in the day when it was even harder to be a trans man, he'd gone down to Trinidad, Colorado and the surgery there. At least that's what he had told her. She couldn't imagine the difficulty of that. Ever since then Josh made a place and offered his generous heart to anyone needing help or someone to listen. "Everyone needs somewhere to go and someone to tell, he said.

The anxiety of not knowing what was going on and a sense of certainty that it was something bad started to spill over into her thoughts. Her eyes darted around looking for cops even though that wasn't part of his message.

Anxious thoughts had haunted her since the moment she received his text. She'd been certain that the plane would crash, that Josh had been taken by the cops, that he would hate her forever for daring to disobey him. He once told her that fear and anxiety we're just weather. They were just our personal downpour, and it would eventually stop. And so one should take an umbrella and do one's best even when the rain of personal drama kept coming.

It took six hours all told to get from the Albuquerque airport to Josh's house in Midtown Memphis.

Josh's door was answered by the most beautiful man she'd ever seen, about five years younger than she was with guileless blue eyes. You could get lost in those eyes, like a ship sailing into the unknown sea, with sensuality like seaweed slipping through and over ocean waves. Miriam stared, and for a brief moment, she imagined tasting salt-kissed lips while watching the sunset wrapped in his strong arms. It was only the forceful worry about Josh that pulled her from the depths of her erotic imagination.

"Who are you?" The words tumbled from her, propelled by the shock of seeing this perfectly formed man framed in Josh's doorway. She fought her strange wild joy of losing herself in his eyes.

It was definitely Josh's house. She could see his slouchy leopard skin chair just beyond the door and the Stieglitz study of hands on the wall. She was touched that he'd kept it. She'd stolen for him early in her apprenticeship, joking that if he kept it, he would always have her hands with him.

She looked around, but she didn't see anyone except this man filling the doorway. No cop cars around the corner. Just him. And her. And what felt like a gulf of questions to be sailed through.

"I could ask you the same," he said. "In fact, I will. Who are you? What are you doing here? And why do you have a suitcase?"

She looked down guiltily at her battered, stuffed overnight bag, more often used for stashing stolen treasures than as a travel tote. It still had mud stains from the time she had to escape by rolling down a slope. From his perspective it must look like she was moving in.

Did he think that Josh and she were lovers? The warmth of a blush suffused her cheeks. Making love to Josh would be like making love to a kind old uncle. But better for him to believe that than for him to know the truth. Still she couldn't help herself as she stole another look down the man's body. Mapplethorpe should have lived to photograph this one.

She scolded herself. Her focus should utterly be on Josh, not on whosever handsome boy toy this was.

Then it connected, her thoughts tumbling a montage of handsome younger men just like this one. They had been in and out of Josh's life in the time she'd studied with him and even more often afterwards. Could this be Josh's lover? But if he was, where was Josh?

"I'm just a friend," she said. "I'm looking for Josh. I—I need to know where he is. Who are you?"

He bit his upper lip and stared into a space above and to her left. Then he looked her up and down, resting on her breasts a bit too long for a gay man with a lover. Eventually, he seemed to come to some sort of decision. He lifted his chin defiantly in the air and she couldn't help but notice the delicacy and length of his lashes. Finally, with a sense of triumph tinging his voice, he said, "A friend? But you're not wearing a hat."

A hat? A friend with a hat? But that was one of Josh's codes. How did this man know the code? And why did he think it referred to a real hat? "I couldn't bring my hat. Josh will understand."

The young man shut the door in her face so quickly and so suddenly that it almost smashed Miriam's toes.

She knocked again and again but the door remained closed. Rage completely out of proportion took over her senses. Her eyes burned in the wet air. She wanted to hit something or someone. Where was Josh? Who was this interloper? What the hell was going on? And how did he know the codes?

She forced herself to calm, taking breath after breath while standing on the porch. She forced herself to study, to be aware, to be a professional thief. The door was new since the last time she was here. The edging strips had been painted recently, but she could see that the door was forced at some point. But not recently. It looked like Josh replaced the Rabson lock with a Poulard. Good choice. Though it was probably why someone had chosen to destroy the door rather than pick it. If it wasn't cops, was it a client? Lord knew he dealt with some real bruisers on occasion.

She reached a curious finger and stroked the brass lock feeling for the chilly metal and the familiar keyhole. It brought back a visceral memory of aching fingers and dry eyes, of the dusty floor she'd sat on during her months of practice with Josh's lock collection until finally she'd managed to open each one and retrieve the game piece within.

She could unlock this one. No problem. But in daylight? With the man watching through the window? No.

She glanced around, taking in as much of the building and the surroundings as she could. They hadn't changed much in the time she'd been away. The leafy Memphis suburb had a rails-to-trails path along the back of the houses. She looped the bag over her shoulder, made a show of walking dejectedly away, and slipped into the trailhead.

Even though it was November, the poison ivy and honeysuckle still twined greenly across trees and fences emitting a verdant moist smell comprised of humus, mold, and the buttery perfume of the creeping plants at her feet. The tree leaves had turned and the canopy was a motley yellow, green, and red.

When she lived here, there had been an entrance protected by thorny devil's walking stick and other noxious plants. Her wool coat would protect her from those, but it would slow her down.

She silently thanked Josh for his insistence that a thief's shoes should always allow one to run or climb. Even her fancy party shoes were practical and now, with the need to climb the hill and wind through vegetation so very different than the desert landscape of Albuquerque, she felt a burst of gratitude toward her ballet flats.

The chain link fence at the back of the house was overrun with vines, mostly poison ivy. He'd promised her that he would remove it, since breathing in the plant could be as harmful to people with sensitivities as brushing up against it. He hadn't. She wrapped her coat tightly around her body and pulled her scarf around her nose to protect herself as best she could. She hadn't been sensitive when she'd first encountered it, but time after time of pushing through the weeds outside Josh's fence changed that fact. Josh needed her and she couldn't help as much if her skin was burning and itching.

Josh's bedroom was on the second floor by the wooden balcony jutting out over the backyard. Back when she was still practicing as a gymnast she shimmied up the supports regularly. Now? Who knew. She had gained a lot of weight in the last decade. Not that she was out of shape, but she mostly ran and lifted weights these days. She couldn't remember the last time she'd practiced this sort of thing. She dropped her bag and her coat at her feet, pulled out her lock picks, and attempted the climb.

OK. That's it. She had to lose the weight. Fifteen pounds might not look like much in an outfit, and it wasn't a huge weight gain, but functionally it made a difference in climbing and acrobatics. It took her two tries but she finally made it to the balcony. She tested the sliding glass doors that were kept locked.

The door slid easily. Her stomach churned as every one of her senses went on high alert. An overpowering reek of ammonia, feces, and old blood made her gag as it filled her nose and mouth. The rug had large blood stain, dried brown, as did the middle of the bed.

Josh! What happened here?

She checked behind the bed and into the closet. She pulled off the covers, seeing more blood. But no body.

Blessed be you, Holy One. Please don't let Josh be dead. Protect him, God.

She returned to built-in dresser in the closet for a more thorough search but found nothing unusual, just Josh's normal colorful wardrobe. The top shelf had something wrapped in a Pride flag, but it turned out to be a small bronze by Dali depicting a woman with drawers as her torso. It was slightly disturbing and not at all Josh's style. She re-wrapped it and put it back. Her eyes pricked, and at the moment she wasn't sure whether it was horror of what had happened here or the smell that was the cause.

She heard a galumphing up the stairs and froze. Then she dropped to her belly behind the bed, hoping she wouldn't be seen. This close to the ground the smell was even worse. Irrelevantly, she wished she had a mint. A very strong mint.

It was the young man, of course. He choked as he entered the room. He began stripping the bed, dropping the bedding on the floor.

Miriam slid on her belly under the bed. But it must have been that action that alerted him to her presence.

He shrieked and then crossed around the bed to see her.

She stood up, tossed her hair, and fixed him with a full-on glare. "Damn you!" she said. "Where is Josh? What have you done with him?"

He shrank back from her fury.

"Nothing. Nothing. He's in the hospital."

"Well if he's in the hospital something happened. Tell me now quickly and I won't hurt you." She leveled a dark glare at him. "Much."

He blinked rapidly and backed up a step. A civilian. Perhaps the boy toy explanation was the best then. But she had to keep him off-balance until she figured out where Josh was and how to help him.

"Tell me your name and why you are in Josh's house. Then tell me what happened to Josh. Do it quickly."

He trembled, which made Miriam feel like a monster. This wasn't her preferred course of action. But there was no time for anything else if Josh was in danger. The only weapons she had were her wits and her presence. She had to use both to save him.

"He's in the hospital."

"So you said before. But that's not an answer. Who are you?"

"Frankie."

Her mouth dropped open. Damn! Him? Was she ever this incompetent as an apprentice? That changed things. Of course, she'd never found her teacher in a pool of blood and shit. Her voice softened. "Did you find Josh, Frankie? Was he bleeding when you found him?"

His eyes filled with tears and he nodded.

"You brought him to the hospital?"

He nodded again.

"OK. I'm Miriam. I used to be named Frankie like you. Understand?"

His eyes widened at that. "You're his apprentice?"

"Not anymore. I chose another name when I set out on my own. But we can catch up later. I need to know what is wrong with Josh."

"They didn't tell me. They just said he had some sort of internal bleeding. He sent me home. Told me to wait."

"Yeah, Josh can be a jerk about hospitals." Her mind was circling itself trying to figure out the next steps. "OK. You clean while I check with the hospital. Which one?"

"Saint Francis."

It took all her charm to make it through the chain, but she finally got in touch with someone who would tell Josh's "sister" what was wrong. Some sort of gastrointestinal bleed out.

Once the sheets were in the washer and Frankie returned to her, she said, "Pack up, we're going to the hospital."

"But he said—"

"I don't care. He's a crazy old coot, but he's our crazy old coot and he needs us there more than he needs us to obey."

JOSH LOOKED SO FRAIL and pale. An IV drip had been connected to his right arm, which dangled over the mattress, his hand resting on the rail.

A plant that must have belonged to a previous occupant drooped on a side table. Its dirt was dry, so Miriam watered it, feeling the need to do something to help, even if all she could help was a dry plant.

A gray curtain separated them from the man in the bed next to Josh's. The man couldn't stop coughing. Miriam couldn't grow accustomed to it. It would start with just a few coughs, a moan, and then a paroxysm of loud, heart-wrenching coughs that ended with him moaning and gasping. The first time it happened she'd raced to the nurses' station, but they said it was the illness and he had what he needed, though a dark-eyed nurse had walked over to check nonetheless.

This wasn't the musical background she would have chosen for Josh, though he still hadn't woken from the surgery, so he likely didn't care.

Frankie kept standing up and pacing around the bed in fits of nerves then coming to sit on the couch next to Miriam. She'd drape her arm over him and say the soothing things she wished someone would say to her. At those times he nestled against her and her body responded. But she simply wove her fingers into his hair and let him lean against her. Strange to be the older one, the one who provides direction and comfort. But here she was. Her mentor needed her and her mentor's apprentice did as well. She bridged the gap.

Nurses entered and left, fragranced with the harsh alcohol scent of hand sanitizer and soap. They checked and promised to return. They'd said that since she was Josh's daughter, she could stay.

For hours Frankie and Miriam stood vigil until finally Josh's eyes fluttered open.

He shook his head in confusion. "Frankie? And Frankie?" Then closed his eyes again and fell back asleep. He did this twice more until he came fully back.

"Miriam? I told you to stay where you were. And Frankie. Why aren't you home?"

"Well surely you sent me that message knowing I'd disobey. If you'd wanted me to stay in Albuquerque, you wouldn't have messaged me. I know your ways, Mr. Miyagi."

He snorted. The man in the next bed seemed to take that as a cue for another coughing attack. When it was quiet again, Josh said, "And now you have corrupted my new Frankie."

She shrugged. "Had to happen sometime. It's good for him. Good for you too. He saved your life, you know."

Frankie stared at her questioningly, and she nodded.

Josh sighed. "Yeah. Doc said that. Thanks. And thank you both for coming." He closed his eyes for a moment. "Now go home, Frankie. You too, Miriam. If you're such a damned balabusta who can't leave well enough alone, you can take charge of Frankie. Teach him something useful."

She didn't move.

"Go," he said. His voice was so weak and so unlike her memories of his strength and command that she blinked back tears.

Miriam gripped his cold frail hand in her own smaller hand and kissed him on the forehead. "You terrified me," she whispered.

"Yeah? Well good. Consider it a lesson."

"In what?"

"Hubris."

Letters of Love and Larceny

The dark outside Crosby's window felt quiet and thick, as if the world had been wrapped in black velvet. It was a seamless, sweet blackness that soothed away the jangle of the day. The hours past midnight belonged to him, even if the days did not.

Crosby felt the paper. Soft, but still a bit stiff. It had a light tan patina that gave it a slightly aged look. But the scent of coffee still emanated from it. That would fade in time. He considered a light toasting in the oven to speed the aging process. But it was already late, and Emily's birthday was tomorrow.

He pulled up the Harvard Library page on his laptop and zoomed in on the letter from Keats to Fanny Brawne. The paper looked like tan cream and the text faded to a beautiful sienna. He wished he could touch it and smell it. Perhaps at some point he would make the trip to Boston, but for now he had to stay in Albuquerque. His job paid barely enough for a one-bedroom apartment over a vegan bakery near Central.

It was a shame that the New Mexico University Library didn't have a collection of Keats's love letters. Or anyone's love letters for that matter. Even Georgia O'Keefe's passionate correspondence with Alfred Stieglitz was stored at the Smithsonian and the Yale Library, leaving her own house and museum to make do with a collection of incoming mail found in her books. Still, he should make a trip to the Ghost Ranch and ask to see her correspondence. There was nothing like really holding a letter to get a sense of it and of her. If they had a love letter from Stieglitz to Georgia O'Keefe, it would make a great addition to his letters to Emily. He hadn't had a vacation day in two years. He could ask for one. Of course, he'd have to make a reservation and that was somewhat chancy.

He focused on the screen zeroing in on the paper again. Was that a slight stain on the middle left side? Perhaps it was the oil from Fanny's thumb. That would be nice. He wondered how he could replicate it.

He picked up a 5/0 sable brush lying on the stained Ikea table and took a tiny drop of brown watercolor. He dropped it into the palette's cup watching as the curling pigment stained the water. He added a bit of yellow and another dollop of brown, mixed it, then compared the color to the oily stain on the image.

Good enough.

He washed the brush in a cup of fresh water before returning it to the pigment, allowing the bristles to soak up his mixture before carefully tapping the paintbrush to splatter droplets onto the paper and watching the capillary action through the paper. When it looked right, he slanted the brush left to stop the drops. He pressed his own thumb into the corner of the paper and thought of Emily, her short dark hair and hazel eyes. He half thought he could press his love for her into the letter as if this were a literary kiss channeling another man's passion for another woman straight into Emily's heart. A capillary magic achieved through pen and ink.

Keats wrote using a steel dip pen, which was fortunately very similar to modern steel calligraphy pens, or at least similar enough that he could get the same effect. He tried it out on a scrap of undyed paper. It looked like it would be about right, just the right thickness at least. Keats' letter started "My Dearest Girl" in delicate, swooping letters. On the scrap, Crosby practiced writing "My Dearest" over and over again until it was so close to Keats's handwriting that no one could tell a difference.

Then, feeling as if he were Keats himself, he changed "Girl" to "Emily" and wrote the entire thing once more. Small divergences in the text might be expected, but the salutation must be perfect. Once it was the best he could manage, he pulled out the prepared letter paper.

He sent up a tiny prayer that it would be done in one without so much as a misplaced drop and dipped his pen in fresh pigment. He bent to the page, a drop of brown bulbing at the end of the tip.

He brought an image of Emily to his mind, her easy smile, her dark glossy hair, the way she smelled of bread and sex and started the first word, the pen scritching along the paper as it must have done for Keats.

His phone rang, breaking the two a.m. silence, and his hand jerked.

Ruined!

Damn. He didn't even have to look at the phone. He knew who it would be. Tara Anne Becker. His double-damned boss demanding something minor that had to be done right then. He considered not answering, but a glance at the large brown blot spreading across the paper confirmed that he would have to start over anyway using another of his precious hand-aged sheets of paper. Besides, Tara would just keep ringing his phone until he responded.

"Hello?"

Even over the phone her voice grated against his ears like a broken pen on rag. "I looked over your latest map. It's just not good enough. I want a redrafted version in my office tomorrow morning. By ten! Understand?"

He didn't, but she hung up before he could ask questions.

MIRIAM

Miriam took another sip of the deep bitter-chocolaty coffee swirled with chiles and cream and topped with cinnamon, holding it within her mouth where it barely burned the inside of her cheeks. The fragrance penetrated her nose from both the inside and the outside for a few moments.

Alluvial Coffee had the best coffee in New Mexico and was one of the only coffee shops that stayed open late, but the chair's hard wood back dug into her back and the table shook a bit with each sip. Not that it mattered. The coffee was that good.

She opened up the bright blue, portfolio folder with the printouts. It was old-fashioned, but Google Drive could be compromised by either the police or by one of her rivals. A home on the dark web left her vulnerable to any jerk with better computer skills than she had, which was just about everyone on the dark web. Paper documents were more secure and could be destroyed without leaving a trace.

She read through the description of the pen again.

The client wanted a Perrier-Jouët Anniversary Edition pen. Made from rose gold and valued at $235,000 each, if you could find one for sale. Only 1,811 had ever been made by the pen maker Omas. She'd had to do her homework to find this one since so few had ever landed on the secondary market. According to her agent, the client was willing to pay a $70,000 "finder's fee" for the pen. Minus a twenty-five percent commission to her agent, that would net a cool $52,500, which wasn't bad for a few weeks research and a little larceny. Plus, who knew what else Dr. Becker kept in that safe.

Miriam cased the doctor's oversized box of a house in Tanoan without finding any evidence of a safe. So, either Becker kept her treasures in her office safe, or they were in a safe deposit box, which was not Miriam's preferred five-finger shopping environment.

She pulled up the folder on Becker, which largely consisted of fawning press that had to have been written by Becker's own publicist and slipped to lazy journalists. The same lie about Becker's childhood poverty kept coming up, but Miriam's own research had turned up a comfortable upper middle-class life. She'd found some pretty awful stuff about her as an employer, borderline illegal anti-employee acts on Glassdoor.com, but nothing precisely actionable. But you don't get a one-star rating on Glassdoor without being horrendous to work for.

Miriam tried to get a feel for the woman. If Miriam were a press-courting, lazy, cruel sociopath with treasures, where would she keep them? Certainly not in a safe deposit box. No. She wouldn't trust another institution to safeguard her treasures. They would be as close to her as possible. Her office. Close to her desk. In a safe.

Miriam spent a month staking out the office until the rhythms were as familiar to her own. At eight a.m., the first smattering of employees arrived. At eight thirty, Tara Becker drove up, parked in the same parking place, and emerged from her car wearing the exact same black dress and dark heels as the day before.

Exactly how many black dresses did the woman own?

Not important. What was important was the fact that no one would be in that office at six thirty a.m., which gave her plenty of time to find and crack the safe.

CROSBY

Crosby locked his bicycle, waved his card key, and made his way to his desk on the eighth floor.

No one else was in the office at 5:30am. The only lights on were the emergency lights, which buzzed with more hostility in the quiet. The sun shimmered with the barest glow to the horizon, the pale blue meeting the darkness in the sky. But it wasn't enough to illuminate any of the offices inside.

It felt drab and inhuman without people. His desk was just outside his boss's office where she required him to act as a receptionist as well as a designer, which meant that all his work was done on the backdrop of non-stop interruptions. He sometimes saw Tara looking at him with a smug smile, as if she were righting all past wrongs by torturing him.

Jobs for designers and especially cartographers were thin on the ground. He'd applied at the USGS, but even if he were willing to move to Colorado or Nevada, where most of the work was done, there were no jobs available. Tara had promised him a referral to the cartographic division of Rolden Gas Exploration, where she held a position on the board of directors. But somehow nothing ever came up. Sometimes when she was angry with him, she told him that he was worthless and would have to tell any future employer that, so he'd better up his game or else. If he could ever get ahead of his debts, he would quit.

He flicked the green glass desk lamp on his elegantly carved receptionists desk Tara bought to "make a statement." The lamp created a cozy pool of golden light in the darkness surrounding him.

Let someone else turn on all the lights on the floor. He preferred the warmth of the desk lamp to the painful fluorescents.

The light revealed the illustrated map he'd created showing all of Rolden Gas' holdings in a comic illustrated form. The map was spread carelessly over the papers and coffee mug on his desk. Angry red notes slashed across the painstakingly drawn buildings with notations like, "This looks stupid" or "Boring!" He studied the buildings she didn't like. There didn't seem to be anything that unified her complaints.

He pulled out a drawing pad to redraft the Rolden tower.

MIRIAM

Miriam had dressed for the cold in a black Polartec hoodie with a balaclava covering her nose and mouth. Early morning in Albuquerque was nippy, though by noon it would warm again. No cars were in the parking lot, though someone had left a bicycle secured to a rack. Probably didn't want to bike home after a long night but best to be careful. She'd parked a block away behind the Starbucks. No point in having someone notice the car.

This building was pretty lightly secured, relying on cheap 125khz EM4100 RFID entry cards, which could be copied with a simple handheld RFID writer, rather than putting out money for a better system. Miriam shook her head. So many businesses were penny smart and dollar dumb.

She'd lifted one of the card keys yesterday and copied it in under a minute before replacing it in the woman's purse. Now, she passed the key fob she'd made in front of the reader, opened the door, and was greeted by a rush of warm air redolent with the scents of dusty industrial carpeting, old cigarettes, and plastic furniture.

She slipped in and stood quietly for a moment listening. But nothing more than the calming buzz of the electric lights and the whoosh of the heat greeted her.

Safe. It looked like no one was here.

Miriam loved office buildings by night when the hordes had abandoned them for their cozy houses. At night the desks revealed their personalities. Each desk was a novel telling stories about its occupant.

She had time, so she checked a few of the desks on her way to the elevator. One was crowded with pictures of children smiling bright smiles together. In other pictures the children dressed as Batman, Superman, and Spider-Man mugged for the camera. Someone who was clearly a much-loved wife was held the smaller kids. The nameplate on the desk read "Willie Roman" so the kids were probably his. A cardboard box dressed up with blue gift wrap paper adorned with a gold bow requested donations to Haven House Shelter on the desk. The nearby brochure asked for donations of items or money to buy supplies for victims of domestic violence. Nice. Willie was clearly a stand-up guy.

Miriam took one of the envelopes from his drawer, fished in her wallet for cash, and placed $218 inside, pushing the money to the bottom of the box, below the packs of socks and underwear where it wouldn't be found until the items were donated.

Maimonides said one of the highest levels of Tzedakah was to give to the poor without knowing who will receive it and without the recipient knowing who has given it. In this way even thieves like Miriam served the interests of heaven. Or at least she liked to think she did, especially near the high holidays when she could use all the favorable attention from the Divine she could get.

For now, though, it was time to serve the interests of her patron by stealing from the filthy rich to sell to the morally deficient rich. Though in this case perhaps they were both morally deficient. She reached the elevator, used her RFID tag to confirm her right to travel to the eighth floor and headed up.

CROSBY

It was Crosby's second cup of bitter office coffee barely improved by the cheap fake creamer. His third redrafting of the building was still crap. Or maybe it wasn't. He couldn't tell anymore.

He wadded up the piece of paper and tossed it with a sense of irritation and satisfaction into his wastepaper basket.

There was no point. Until Tara told him what she needed he wouldn't be able to produce it. The one that he had given her still looked the best. He laid his head on the desk feeling its cool surface calming his brain.

If he couldn't make the map work, perhaps he could work on the letter for Emily.

He'd brought a printout of the letter from Keats to Fanny Brawne with him. He might as well give it a try and see if he could at least get the salutation. Practice, practice, practice. He wrote again this time on a sheet of white paper using a fountain pen because it was all he had at the office, "My Dearest Emily"

The pen slipped along the paper smoothly without a single scritch and he felt Keats hand guiding his. He felt Keats's words filling him. When he copied, "My love has made me selfish. I cannot exist without you — I am forgetful of every thing but seeing you again — my Life seems to stop there — I see no further" he could feel Keats in his heart. Fanny looked like Emily to him and his longing for her became all-encompassing as he wrote.

He looked down at the words drying on the page. It was very close. Very, very close. All he needed to do was iron out some of his own writing quirks.

He rolled the fountain pen in his hand with pleasure. It was a smooth black jobber far easier to use than the steel calligraphy pen. With an internal barrel and the smooth gold tip, it was beautiful.

All pens are all beautiful. Even a disposable plastic pen has its own beauty because it is the source of so much creativity. Pens were the actual source of civil society, the origin of law, justice, art, literature and everything else precious. This fountain pen was one of the very few luxuries he brought to work.

His love of fountain pens, one of the few points of commonality between him and Tara, provided the sole bit of companionship between them. Tara made sure to show him each expensive fountain pen she bought before carefully placing it in the safe. He suspected that she wanted him envious and cowed, but in truth it was a sensual pleasure to feel a pen in his hands. Even if he could never own a thousand-dollar pen, just being able to touch it was special.

He looked again at the letters he had drawn using the fountain pen and considered. If he could simply get the right color of sepia ink, perhaps he could use a fountain pen to do the work. It would be easier if slightly less exact than the watercolor mixture he'd prepared. Though he wouldn't be dipping his pen as Keats had. Would it separate him from feeling as Keats did when he burned for Fanny Brawne?

But with a fountain pen, he had a chance of getting it done. He just needed the right ink. He considered looking in Tara's office. When he'd last organized her inks, she had six different varieties of sepia. One of them would surely work. Otherwise, the only other choice would be to order it. That would delay the project. He would fail Emily.

He balanced the wrongness of stealing the ink with... He stopped that thought.

No! Righteous fury filled him followed by a sudden realization. He was not stealing. He would borrow the ink.

He was not a thief. It was Tara who stole his life away minute by minute, late-night phone call by late-night phone call, cruelty by cruelty. A sense of justice grew within him, a sense that he deserved that ink. It was the least that she could do.

He muttered to himself, "God, give me a sign if this is the right thing to do," then crossed himself and bowed his head.

Hearing nothing immediately from the Almighty, he turned his attention to the door, which looked like any other office door in its dullness. A standard, light-weight office door that was usually open when Tara was here, the better to watch everyone.

He got up to check the knob and found it locked. Disappointing, but not surprising. And, in a way, it was perhaps the sign from God that he didn't want him taking the ink, even if it wasn't stealing. Not to recommend anything to the Almighty, but he might want to look to reforming Tara's character and not just his own. Not that he was complaining.

Very well, then, he would get back to practicing with the black ink in his fountain pen. Perhaps he could sneak out early and finish Emily's birthday present before they left for the restaurant tonight.

Sinking into copying the letter felt like climbing into bed with a lover. Fanny Brawne tonight, but perhaps Emily soon. This would be the third famous love letter he'd copied for her. It felt intimate to write inside another person's words, erotic and joyous. His practice paper was merely white office paper and the ink black. The fountain pen was subtly wrong in his hand for this document, but it was still coming through. He was connecting to the words, the past, and his future with Emily.

He was so tightly integrated into the words that it was only after he'd written Keats' immortal "Love is my religion — I could die for that — I could die for you. My Creed is Love and you are its only tenet — You have ravish'd me away by a Power I cannot resist" that he became aware of a woman's breath behind him.

He froze.

The breath wasn't Tara's, they were too light for that, too feminine.

Not Emily's. He knew Emily's breath like he knew his own.

He shuddered. If he looked up, would he see Fanny Brawne? Had he summoned her? It could not be.

His breath caught.

MIRIAM

Miriam crept into Tara's reception area silent as a lynx. A man was bent over a desk, a brown lock of hair swinging gently across his brow as he worked copying an old page from an image on his computer screen. He hadn't seen her. Yet.

She held her breath for a moment, uncertain what to do.

His desk, an elegant carved rosewood seemed out of place in the otherwise plain receptionist's space. Too big.

Frustratingly, it was the way of Tara's office door. Someone was showing off and judging by the man at the desk it wasn't him.

Miriam looked at the sheet of paper he was laboring over and glanced over at the screen. An old-fashioned, hand-written letter was displayed at the top. As she quietly observed him, assessing the distance from corridor to the door behind the desk, she came to a decision. She couldn't get past him without being noticed, even as focused as he appeared to be.

Why was he here? She looked again at the page he copied, back at the screen, and then the pieces fell into place.

CROSBY

"You're a forger." A sweet voice with a slight Southern twang broke through Cosby's concentration.

His head jerked up and he released the breath he'd been holding. Not Fanny Brawne. Thank God.

She slid closer to him. Her fragrance of vanilla and leather tickled his nose. "How long have you been forging documents?

"I'm not a forger!"

She motioned toward the letter. "Forgery. And a damned good one. Except for the paper, of course. If you actually want to replicate the letter, you'll need to do something about the paper."

"I know that. I have aged paper at home." An amused glint flashed in her eye. Damn, why did he have to say that? Now she surely thought the worst of him.

"I would have expected no less from a man with your expertise," she said soberly, though her eyes danced with amusement. She motioned at the map bleeding in slashes from Tara's red pen. "Is that your work? It's quite impressive. Especially working here in this environment. The interruptions must drive you crazy. I don't know many people who could do work this good in these conditions."

He knew he was being soft-soaped, though for what purpose? Had Tara sent her to get some sort of blackmail evidence on him? Was this a trap? He should just shut up. He knew that. But he pushed on stubbornly, wanting this attractive woman to understand.

"It's not a forgery. I'm not trying to fool anyone. See, that's my girlfriend's name, Emily." He pointed to the top of the letter on the computer screen, "The original doesn't have her name."

There. Let her process that. Imagine accusing him of forgery. He studied the woman. She was pretty, with long chestnut hair that any artist would want to draw, and she wore a warm black coat and black tights. She could have a microphone in the coat pockets. Or really anywhere.

She bent over, looked at carefully at both the original on the screen and his work, and made a humming sound, nodding as if impressed. "The handwriting is the same. It's a perfect match. Exquisite!"

He blushed, his soul drinking up the compliment. Whatever her motivation was, his soul had starved for too long for someone to see his skill for what it was. Even Emily didn't really understand the work that went into these gifts. And here was this... woman. What was she? And why was she here? He sniffed gruffly. "Not perfect." He pointed to a couple of minor imperfections.

She bent over, a lock of dark hair falling from her hood. It smelled like lavender, vanilla, and something a bit wild.

She nodded thoughtfully. He waited for her mockery, but it didn't come. Instead, her voice seemed tinged with respect when she said, "Your work is as perfect as any forger I've ever known. This looks like a love letter. What is it for?"

"For Emily, my girlfriend. It's her birthday today. I promised her something special. I planned to take her out. I planned to give her this letter. I planned—"

He pressed his hands over his eyes, realizing that he was going to ruin her birthday and not for the first time. Damn Tara! He would lose his job today. Then what would happen to him?

He pressed his palms into his eyelids until the little star effects started. He pulled back emotional control. He sounded whiny, but God he was so tired and there was simply no way he could get this done in time for her birthday. No way in hell.

He slumped, defeated by the complications. If he were honest with himself, it was all his fault for leaving the calligraphy to the last minute. But it had taken weeks to find just the right letter to copy and then additional time to get the paper aged correctly. Through those weeks Tara had pulled him into work for one thing or another nearly every night and weekend. It was almost as if she knew and was trying to sabotage his relationship. But she couldn't know. He hadn't told anyone.

"Go on, what's the problem?" The woman said in a soft voice, "Tell me. My name is Miriam. Maybe I can help."

"My boss," he said, his voice neutral as he watched her face seeking an answer as to whether she was Tara's cat's-paw. If she were, she'd already learned enough to give his boss even leverage over him. He wondered if he would turn out like—

His phone pinged with a message. Miriam looked at the screen with unabashed curiosity. It read, "You had better be in the office and working or I will make you regret you were ever born."

"Charming," Miriam said. Your girlfriend or your boss?"

"Emily would never be that way. She's the sweetest person you've ever met."

"So, your boss?" Miriam asked.

He nodded glumly. "Yeah."

"Doesn't sound like you've got the greatest relationship with her. From what I've heard, no one does." Her voice was soft and sympathetic and for reasons he couldn't explain to himself, he found himself telling her everything about his boss, about his finances, about this one last chance to impress Emily, to propose to her. He even told her about not having the ink he needed and that his boss hoarded more than she could ever use in her drawer.

When the torrent of words sputtered to a stop, Miriam patted him lightly on his hand. Her touch felt so warm. so kind, almost like Emily's. Tears welled in his eyes. God, if this is your sign, can't you be a little more explicit? What do you want me to do?

Miriam seemed to struggle for a moment and then said, "I think I can help you solve your problem, and you can help me solve mine."

"How is that?"

"I can open the door to Tara Becker's office to let you get the ink. But you can't tell anyone I was here. Understand?"

"Really? You have the key?"

"In a way. Let me show you. But it's our secret, OK? I need you to give me your promise."

That's when it hit him. She wasn't Tara's tool. She was a thief. A real thief. And he had a choice to make.

A voice echoed down the hall. "Hey? Is someone here? Hello?"

It took less time for Miriam to open the lock with her picks than it took him to open his house door with a key. She slipped into Tara's office just as Shaw, the database administrator walked into the room.

"Hey, what are you doing here this early? Or late? Does the ogre have you working this late?" Shaw was a wiry man who spent every break from work prepping for his latest marathon.

"She called me in to work on a map."

"You mean she screamed at you, told you that you wouldn't amount to anything and made you come in to fix a bunch of nonsense?"

"You too?"

He shrugged. "Just part of the job, I guess. I've never understood why you don't just quit. She treats you worse than anyone here. You pee in her oatmeal or what?"

"I don't know why she has it in for me. She's a bad one though. I signed a non-compete when I got here. I never imagined that it meant I would never be able to work in my field again." Crosby could hear Miriam moving in the other room. He picked up the map and rattled it a bit to cover the sound. What was he going to do?

"She got you by the short and curlies?"

"Pretty much." He could turn Miriam in, pretend that he found her stealing, but then what? Tara might be pleased enough with him to give him a raise, but he knew it wouldn't be much and she was never going to change her stripes.

"I feel for you, man. You're too nice a guy for this world. Just remember, she isn't ever going to stop hurting you. She gets off on it."

He nodded. Who was he if he stayed?

MIRIAM

Miriam's stomach turn over. Out of habit she looked for hiding places and escape hatches, but this office was just an office. There wasn't so much as an executive toilet.

She located the safe, attached the robotic combination genie, and waited. It would take a good ten minutes.

Five minutes into the wait, Crosby walked in. He looked a bit dazed.

"Hey thanks for not turning me in," she said. "I owe you for that."

"I still could."

She nodded. "Tell me, with your skills you could modify the non-compete contract and be free and clear. Why don't you?"

"It wouldn't matter. They're all electronic these days. I'm not a computer tech. Shaw could do it. But I doubt he would. His every transaction is tracked through the system." He bit his lip and stared at Miriam. "What are your plans?"

"I'm going to get what I came for and skedaddle." She thought about the situation. She knew that he would be the primary suspect once she left. She couldn't do much about that, but she could help in other ways. "I might know someone who could make use of your unique talents. Once you get through this situation. My recommendation is that you sit tight. How often does your boss check her safe?"

"Once a month, if that."

"OK. Wait two weeks and then come to me. I'll get you in touch with someone who will pay a lot for your mind and hands."

"I'll think about it. Can you grab the sienna inks for me? You're wearing gloves."

CROSBY

Just a few of our closest friends at the wedding rehearsal dinner, Emily's mother had said. But in looking around at the guests, Crosby saw that he was marrying into crowds of friends and relatives. It was overwhelming. The room pulsed with people, with their conversations, with their bodies all of it crammed into the Montague's back dining room, which boasted New Mexican-Italian fusion cuisine. From what he could tell, that meant spaghetti topped with tomato sauce and green chilies, which fragranced the room with spice and olive oil.

Emily looked radiant tonight. Her lips, which were nearly always touched with smiles seemed beatific tonight. Her hair bounced as she spoke animatedly with each person she spoke with.

For his part, Crosby couldn't believe she'd said yes. He wished with one part of himself that they didn't have to wait for the wedding, that he could carry her away with him into someplace quiet and private. But that would wait until tomorrow night, to the honeymoon. In the meantime he now had more friends through marriage than he'd ever had.

He felt a familiar breath from behind him. Miriam could sneak as quietly as she wanted. It didn't matter. He would know her breath anywhere.

"Miriam! Thank you for coming. Will we see you at the wedding tomorrow?"

She pulled him into a hug, and he breathed in her scent of lavender and vanilla. "Sorry, no. Business calls. But I have a present for you," she whispered. "But you can't tell anyone."

"I have a present for you as well, and you can tell everyone." He winked and pulled a box from behind the gifts table.

Her eyes widened as she gazed on the replica of the illuminated Golden Haggadah, the section known as Miriam's Dance. She fingered it and then pulled her eyes away. "It is very fine work. You are the best at what you do."

"It's nice to have artistic challenges along with the mundane work you send my way." In truth, the biggest artistic challenges, and the most lucrative, were often the corporate and government documents that he forged for her. Compared to that, writing the odd love letter or illuminated manuscript or a fantasy map, when he got one, were easy days.

Emily turned to see them and smiled warmly. "Miriam! Thank you so much for coming. I can't tell you how grateful we are that your friend needed a fantasy mapmaker. Who knew fantasy maps paid that much, huh?"

"Just glad I could help. When Crosby said he wanted a new life with shorter hours, well, what are friends for if not to put them together with other friends. I do think that Crosby does the best fantasy documents I've ever seen. They look so real."

"I know! Did you ever see the love letters he sent me?"

Miriam coughed to cover a laugh. "I may have seen one in progress."

"They're all replicas of historical love letters. Except with my name inserted. It's amazing! When we get our new house, I want to frame them."

Miriam placed a slender box wrapped in silver paper in his hands and whispered to Crosby, "Open this in private."

He wrapped his fingers around it, sure that he knew what it was. So it was that one of the rarest of fountain pens, from the

Montblanc Love Letter series honoring Keats that he'd last seen in Tara's safe, ended up in the locked drawer of Crosby's desk.

Five Finger Teamwork

M iriam, her brown hair bound into a ponytail bobbing
along her back, loped through the cottonwoods growing
wild near the Rio Grande Bosque trail. Step, bounce, step,
bounce. Golden leaves fluttered against a true blue sky, and the
tannic, dusty, ozone smell of Albuquerque filled her lungs. The
morning had been so cold that she'd considered wearing tights
instead of shorts, but as she ran, the sun warmed the path. Tights
would have been too much. Her backpack was beginning to feel
too warm as it was.

Some kind soul had thoughtfully painted all the tree roots
bright yellow a long time ago. They'd faded and been covered
with the gray volcanic dust, but it was still possible to see them.
She made a little game of bounding over each hazard, ever
mindful of the time. Once she was doing the actual job, and
not just this practice run, she would have fifteen minutes to go
from Tingley Beach along the Bosque to the house, find the cast
bronze octopus floating on a sea of malachite, and make it out
between the time the Lissons' maid left for her day off and the
security officer arrived on his rounds.

In darkness.

Hopping the roots helped her remember their locations. At
least she hoped it would. At any rate, it was fun. And if a job
wasn't fun, what was the point? She took off through the trees
heading north. She passed a slender woman with a box of cookies
and a stuffed toy around a huge camera lens waiting, presumably,

for the family to show up for their photograph. The Bosque was a favored place for photographers as well as cyclists, runners, children engaged in fake sword fights, and expert thieves keeping in shape.

As Miriam jogged past the small boardwalk overlooking the Rio Grande, she spotted one of the loveliest women she'd ever seen curled up and crying on the ground. The woman's chestnut hair fanned out around a red wool coat that had been laid flat, cushioning the bare wood. She glanced at her watch. Damn. She'd have to try to time the run again later today. Though she'd already timed it a few times in the last week. But having one last dress rehearsal gave her a bit of extra confidence when engaged in a spot of larceny.

She pressed the hold on the Garmin's timer and jogged over to investigate. Maybe a homeless woman? But the woman was well-dressed and well-fed. If she was homeless, she hadn't been on the streets long enough for the rough life to affect her. Miriam knelt down. There were bruises on the woman's arms in the shape of a man's fingers and a shiner that looked like she'd been punched.

She made her voice as soft and gentle as she could. "Hey, can I help?"

The woman shrank away, her long eyelashes blinking away tears rapidly. Despite her apparent anguish and the clear evidence of being beaten, the woman looked like an athlete. Perhaps a dancer with her long legs and beautiful features?

"I'm not going to hurt you. Come on, let's get you up on the bench. Would you like some coffee?" Miriam reached into her backpack and pulled out her thermos. She had to fill her backpack with something to simulate the weight of the statuette, and the thermos was the perfect size and weight. And if one is going to carry a thermos anyway, why not fill it with latte? "Here, have some. It will help. I promise. Caffeine is magic." She unscrewed the top and took in a deep breath of that magic.

The woman reached for the coffee and gulped it down. "Thank you, so much. It's exactly what I needed." She offered the cup back to Miriam, who refilled it and handed it back to her.

"Have a bit more. For medicinal purposes."

The woman laughed, and it was a warm laugh with a bitter edge, like the latte she was drinking. "Isn't that an expression for whiskey?"

"I don't have any whiskey with me. Sorry about that. What's your name? I mean if we're going to be drinking buddies, we probably should know each other's names. I'm Miriam."

"Jessie, like Jessie James, except I'm a girl and I don't rob banks." It was clearly a well-worn line.

Miriam laughed, joining in the joke. "OK, Jessie, you look like you've been run over by a truck of fists. Can I help you get home?"

Jessie's face crumpled. "I don't have a home. Not anymore."

"Your man do this to you?" She motioned to the bruises.

"Yes. No. It don't matter. Those are my doing. More like war wounds than domestic violence."

"Mm-hmm." Miriam let her left eyebrow raise just enough to let Jessie know she wasn't taken in. "You might want to consider classes in self-defense."

"No need."

"Mm-hmm. I have a small place not too far from here. You're welcome to stay there tonight while you figure something out. We can find some whiskey or ibuprofen, whatever works."

"Both, please."

Miriam helped her up and guided her to the elegant Huning Castle apartment she was generously house-sitting for the absent owners, albeit without their knowledge. She was sure they would be grateful to have their place guarded so ably, especially since they hadn't invested in a good security system.

Jessie looked up at the apartment building. "Wow! I'd heard that these apartments were waitlisted clear into the next century. Who are you sleeping with to get a place here?"

"A woman with a plan doesn't need to sleep around. I got a real estate license upon moving to Albuquerque. So I'm first to get the information on people who need renters or house-sitters."

That was true, as far as it went. Realtors had the keys to the castle, even Huning Castle. It really opened up opportunities. So many places to visit. So many keys available. So much information. Though Miriam hadn't seen the point in going through formal processes to house-sit. Just pick someone who clearly needed her and give their apartment her love and attention. Right now the Rodriguez place was her home while they vacationed in Malaysia.

Given a choice, Miriam preferred her "house-sitting clients" to have a home designed by a prominent decorator. This one was. The round glassed-in living room had a Noguchi coffee table with dark wood legs as a signature piece in the center surrounded by a pink sofa and chairs. None of the items in the room were particularly valuable, but they were all done with an eye toward beauty and luxury.

Jessie gasped as she entered. "This is your place?"

"For a while. I'm house-sitting. My friends are in Malaysia." Best to stick as close to the truth as possible. "Make yourself at home. There's a second bedroom over there with a private bath if you would like to shower. I'll see if I can rustle up some ibuprofen and bandages."

"And whiskey?"

"Sure." Miriam had no idea where the Rodriguezes kept their whiskey, or even if they drank, but she prepped a pot of tea, just in case, and then sat down to study the plans for the Lisson house. It was west of the Albuquerque Country Club in a posh neighborhood near the Bosque. Like many wealthy people, the Lissons had bragged a bit too much about their newest acquisition, a Cast Bronze Octopus Over Malachite with precious gems studded through it by Studio Greytak. The auction house records listed its previous sale as $125,000.

Miriam knew John Macsofor would flip for this piece. He loved anything ridiculously expensive and related to the sea. Plus he could be relied upon to buy it quietly and hold it quietly at his home in Queens until the hubbub died down. He wouldn't find anything like this in New York. It really was true that New Mexico was the best place to shop for art. Lots of great bargains and the level of security wasn't all that good, allowing Miriam to leverage her own personal five-finger discount.

The shower stopped and Miriam waited for Jessie to return. When she didn't, Miriam checked on the woman and found her sound asleep sprawled on her stomach on the bed.

That was convenient. Jessie was still asleep a few hours later when Miriam dressed and left for the Bosque.

She moved quietly through the trees, checking back behind her several times without seeing anyone. But her back tingled like someone was watching her. She'd made it most of the way to the Lissons' house when that overwhelming sensation could no longer be ignored.

There was a rustle behind her. Miriam turned, but not fast enough. A blade sliced through her sleeve. Damn! Blood will be obvious to the camera. She squeezed her arm as the assailant turned to try again. Then in a swirl of motion too fast for her to understand, the man was on the ground, his knife was six feet away, and Jessie was on top of him, punching him out until he was still.

"You OK?" Jessie asked.

"What are you doing here?"

"Couldn't sleep."

"So you followed me?"

"Looked like you were heading off for some off-the-clock shopping. Thought I'd tag along. Maybe pick up something for me as well."

Miriam smiled. "Nice work. It looks like you saved my life. But I'm kind of on a timer."

"Of course. I'll wait here. Keep this one from following you."

"Thanks." There wasn't much time to do more than wave at Jessie much less figure out the woman's motives or question her further. She'd lost five minutes. She put on the speed, running through the woods, hopping over the roots. She nearly stumbled a few times, but she kept herself from falling. The blood streaming down her left arm would show up on the camera. She tried to remember the layout from the real estate map. If she was right, the statuette would be in the front room on a bookcase.

Ten minutes. She took two minutes opening the lock and let herself in.

She pulled out her phone and switched on the light app, swinging it toward where she'd seen the statuette a month ago. Now in its place was a large fake book. She opened it, but it was filled with gourmet chocolate bars. Damn.

Seven minutes left. She crammed two of the chocolate bars into her pack and moved the light around the room. It would catch the motion detector, but with any luck the video would identify her as headlights. The outfit she wore was designed to fool the video cameras.

Five minutes left and the Greytak sculpture wasn't in the living room. No time to search every room. She called up the floor plan she'd filched from the Realtor site. Not likely in the bathrooms. Not in the maid's room. The primary bedroom? Worth a try.

The primary bedroom had statuettes! Dear God did it have statuettes. They filled every flat surface and several shelves.

Three minutes left.

She didn't dare turn on a light. It would destroy the carefully wrought illusion her clothing was meant to sustain. If the blood didn't mess that up.

Two minutes left. Was that the soft humming of the security agency's car? The headlights raked through the room. She dropped to the ground and froze. And in that moment, illuminated by the headlights, she spotted a tall bronze octopus hidden between a group of stone landscape sculptures. It was one of the ugliest things Miriam had ever seen that was supposed to be high art.

Why wasn't the car moving on? She squatted there for another hundred hours—or something like that—before he moved on.

She let out a breath, grabbed the octopus, and placed it carefully in the batting in her pack.

Then she slipped back out through the front door and walked sedately through the neighborhood. The cameras on the nearby houses would detect her, but if the clothing worked, they would ignore her as a random vehicle. If anyone saw her, she was just a resident out for a stroll. Once safely beyond the perimeter of the houses, she slipped off the hoodie and placed it in the backpack for extra cushioning, then jogged back to the Bosque and picked up Jessie, who was good to her word and waiting for her. The attempted murderer was on the ground, his breathing shallow.

"How did you do this?" Miriam asked, pointing at the man.

Jessie shrugged. The motion showed off the musculature in her shoulders. "I'm a black belt in six different forms of martial arts."

"Then how did this happen?" She gently touched the red handprint on Jessie's upper arm.

"Let's just say that when someone is as well trained as you are and has seventy pounds of muscle on you, martial arts don't even things up as much as they advertise."

MIRIAM WAITED PATIENTLY. It took a week before Jessie gained the confidence to leave whereever she'd holed up and signal to Miriam that she wanted to talk.

They met on the boardwalk. Miriam set out two small purple cakes and two earthenware mugs and poured each of them large cafe lattes. Miriam smiled as Jessie inhaled the marvelous aroma of chocolate, coffee, and caramel and sighed happily.

"One thing I don't understand," Jessie said, "how did you know when the patrols came through and where the security cameras were?"

Miriam took a long sip of her coffee, swirling it in her mouth as she studied Jessie. Finally she said, "I scoped out the house last month and watched the security patrols going by at four a.m., same time every weekday. I hung out in my car, drinking tea and waiting. Their house had seven security cameras around the perimeter, and I could see two inside. Which meant that the family was pretty confident about their security measures. If they've paid that much for cameras and patrols, they figure thieves will rob poorer houses." She laughed. "Rich people get cocky."

"But you must have known how to avoid the cameras. That was always our gang's problem: finding all the cameras and then disabling them."

"You don't need to disable cameras. You need to be someone else, or preferably several someone elses. Or something else. Cameras are dumb." Miriam smiled as she thought of the hoodie and tights with anti-surveillance fabric designed to fool cameras. What most people didn't know was that ContraSpy Fashion had another line, one designed for those who needed it most: anti-government activists.

Miriam had helped get the product where it needed to go, and in return Jan, the owner, gave her a camera-defying body suit. Not that she planned to tell anyone that. They could do their own research. Instead she regarded Jessie, making her voice stern. "But I've given you a lot of information. How do I know you aren't going to head back to your gang?"

Jessie shuddered and wrapped her arms around her knees. "Not a chance."

"Well, what are your plans?"

"I actually hadn't made any plans beyond just getting away from them. I don't even know where I'm going to sleep tonight." Jessie looked miserable and small, despite her long legs and muscular arms.

"You saved me back there and you helped with the mission. You can stay at my place while you figure things out."

Her beautiful lashes grazed her cheeks and tears welled up. "That's so nice, but you don't even know me."

"I was you once." She patted Jessie's hand gently. "Stay for a while. Help me out and we'll see where this goes. I could use a bodyguard, and you're pretty damn good."

Jessie smiled. "Sure. I'd like that."

Acknowledgements

Much thanks to my wonderful editor Jennifer Lopez of Mistress Editing for her precise editing.

Thanks also go to Eva Papier and Max Roprez for their unflagging support as I wrote;

To Dean Wesley Smith for his invaluable lessons;

And to my husband, Steve, who is always there for me.

Don't miss out!

Visit the website below and you can sign up to receive emails whenever Carolyn Ivy Stein publishes a new book. There's no charge and no obligation.

https://books2read.com/r/B-A-LKYI-WWHUB

Connecting independent readers to independent writers.

Also by Carolyn Ivy Stein

The Adventures of Miriam the Thief
Sweet Lifts

Standalone
Lightning Scarred

Watch for more at www.carolynivystein.com.

About the Author

Carolyn Stein is a freelance writer and editor. She has contributed articles to The Sea in World History book set, Atlas Obscura website, and other publications. She writes historical, fantasy, and science fiction as well as non-fiction and gaming supplements. When not writing she games and experiments with gourmet vegan cooking.

Read more at www.carolynivystein.com.